The Luckiest Leprechaun

by Justine Korman
illustrated by Denise Brunkus

Troll
BridgeWater Paperback

For Ron, my greatest treasure
—J. K. F.

In remembrance of Naava and her many charms
—D. B.

Text copyright © 2000 by Justine Korman.
Illustrations copyright © 2000 by Denise Brunkus.

Published by BridgeWater Paperback, an imprint and trademark of Troll Communications L.L.C.

Published in hardcover by BridgeWater Books.

Design credits are shared by Denise Brunkus, Dorit Radandt, and Shi Chen.

Printed in the United States of America.

10 9 8 7 6 5 4 3

Library of Congress Cataloging-in-Publication Data

Korman, Justine.
The luckiest leprechaun / by Justine Korman; illustrated by Denise Brunkus.
p.   cm.
Summary: When a leprechaun reluctantly lets a dog befriend him, he finds out what it's like to care about someone.
ISBN 0-8167-6604-5 (lib. bdg.)   ISBN 0-8167-6866-8 (pbk.)
[1. Leprechauns Fiction. 2. Dogs Fiction. 3. Friendship Fiction.]
I. Brunkus, Denise, ill. II. Title.
PZ7.K83692Lu   1999
[E]—dc21   99-37016

MacKenzie O'Shamrock, at your service. But you can call me Mac. I'm a leprechaun —and I don't care if you believe in me or not. Get too close and I'll show you who's real with my hammer! I may be small, but we leprechauns are not to be trifled with!

There, now that that's settled, pull up a toadstool, or a chair if you're too big, and I'll tell you my story.

I was born beneath a fairy hill back when time was new. Ever since, I've been making shoes for the fairy folk—and guarding my gold from greedy people!

Treasure hunters have to get up pretty early in the morning to get the best of MacKenzie O'Shamrock! And since leprechauns work at night and sleep during the day, I'm up much earlier than most. No, they haven't made the human yet who could outsmart me!

Then people found a new way to boil my potatoes: They stopped believing in leprechauns! They believed in all sorts of nonsense, but the little man making shoes beneath their very own hedge "couldn't possibly exist." It got so only children and oddballs, like Professor Chester, believed in me.

I didn't need people anyway. I had a nice home under a tree in a quiet park. As long as I had my gold and my work, this leprechaun was content.

Every night, I cobbled for the fairies. Since all the little things do is dance and lose their shoes, business was steady.

Every morning, I'd pack away my tools and curl up in my cozy bed.

And that's just what I was doing one fine morning when I heard a horrible scratching overhead. Dirt poured down on my favorite armchair, as a pair of giant paws burst through the ceiling. My thimble collection clattered to the floor.

I grabbed my hammer and ran outside to see who was wrecking my home! I expected a goblin or some other horrible monster . . .

. . . I found a shaggy red dog burying a stinky soup bone.

"Hello!" she barked. "Who are you?"

"I'm MacKenzie O'Shamrock!" I shouted. "And you . . . you . . . you've got some nerve destroying my home! You'll not be stealing my gold, you mangy mortal! So just take your bone and go!"

"I'm sorry. I didn't realize anyone was living here," the dog said. "Is that your gold? It's very pretty."

"Go!

"Shoo!

"GET LOST!" I shouted.

The dog didn't budge. Shaking her head she said, "I feel terrible. I've got to make this up to you. I'll fix your house. I'll be your guard dog."

"I don't need a guard," I said.

"But you must need a friend. Everyone needs friends," the dog said. "My name is Lucky. What's yours?"

That made me even madder. "MacKenzie O'Shamrock!" I yelled.

"Oh, that's right. You did tell me," Lucky replied. "But that's so much to remember. May I just call you Mac? I hope we'll be friends. Everything's more fun when you do it together, don't you think? Just the other day I . . ."

Lucky would have gone on like that for hours. But I told her to go away and stay away.

Apparently *stay* was the only command the dumb dog knew! From then on, wherever I went, there was Lucky. She was slobbering over me when I woke up at dusk. She was on my heels while I gathered cobwebs for thread.

Lucky even tailed me when I made my deliveries to the fairies.

And she always had a cheerful word—or a hundred. It drove me nuts!

That dog was even happy when it rained.

"Rain is where rainbows come from," Lucky said. "I love rainbows. Don't you? I could chase them all day."

"Why don't you go chase them—so I can get some quiet around here?" I growled.

After a while, Lucky learned not to talk so much—especially when I first woke up in the evening. I won't say we became friends. But she got to be slightly less annoying.

Speaking of annoying, remember that human I mentioned a while back, the oddball who believed in leprechauns? That's right, Professor Chester. Well, he started snooping around my park!

"He's after my gold!" I cried.

"Maybe he just wants to be friends," Lucky suggested.

I snorted. "Humans want only one thing from a leprechaun—gold! But he won't get the best of MacKenzie O'Shamrock!"

Professor Chester was getting dangerously close. He even found a fairy shoe!

"Don't worry, Mac," said Lucky. "You've got your guard dog, remember? I won't let anything happen to your gold."

I took no comfort in the mutt's ravings.

I watched Professor Chester poring over his books of leprechaun lore. "If only I could prove their existence . . ." he muttered.

I shuddered.

"Maybe he'll just go away," Lucky said.

I thought about packing up. But I liked my cozy life under the tree. Besides, business was good, and it's not so easy to find a park filled with fairies.

Then, one day while I was sleeping, the professor found my tree! He was about to capture me and would have gotten my gold for sure when . . .

. . . "WOOF! WOOF! WOOF!" Lucky came charging out of the woods!

The professor cried, "Help! Monster! Help!" He dropped his map and ran off screaming.

I thought I was having a nightmare. I rolled over with a groan and fell right back to sleep.

Professor Chester just kept running until he wore out the soles of his shoes. Turned out the professor was scared of dogs!

That evening, I woke up feeling something was wrong. For one thing, the dumb dog wasn't licking my face. Suddenly, with a jerk, I remembered the nightmare. I checked for my gold in all my secret hiding places. It was gone—and so was Lucky.

I called Lucky's name until my voice was hoarse, but there was no answer! I felt as if I had lost my shadow, and my friend.

Then it hit me—my worst fear had come true! The dog wasn't as silly as she seemed. Lucky had duped me into trusting her. As soon as I'd let down my guard, she'd run off with my gold! I, MacKenzie O'Shamrock, the smartest leprechaun of them all, had finally been tricked out of my treasure.

I searched the park for hours, but there was no sign of my gold or of Lucky.

I told myself the dog had skipped off with my treasure. But part of me didn't believe it. One minute I was furious, the next I was worried. What if the stupid pooch had chased a rainbow into traffic or gotten herself taken to the pound?

I couldn't even keep my mind on my missing gold.

By dawn, I was the saddest leprechaun in the world. After centuries of being suspicious, I'd finally opened my heart and—POW! The first friend I'd made had stolen my gold!

The sun came up and I wiped away a tear.

Then a voice behind me said, "Why are you crying?"

I turned and saw Lucky—and my gold!

"Where were you?" I yelled. "I was worried sick!"

Lucky licked my face. "You do care! I knew we'd be friends!"

I wiped the dog slobber from my face and grumbled, "I was worried about my gold."

Lucky explained that she'd seen Professor Chester nosing around near my tree. After she'd chased him away, she'd hidden my treasure in the tool shed, just to make sure it was safe. Then, worn out from the excitement, she'd fallen asleep.

"Did you really spend all night looking for me?" Lucky asked.
"And the gold!" I added hastily.
But the damage was done. The dog knew I cared—
and she wouldn't stop wagging her tail over it.

So there's my story:

Leprechaun gets gold.

Leprechaun gets dog.

Leprechaun loses gold.

Leprechaun admits that a loyal friend is worth more than gold—as long as the friend doesn't slobber too much.

Now if that isn't a tale worth telling upon a toadstool, I'm sure I don't know what is!